minedition

English edition published 2017 by Michael Neugebauer Publishing Ltd., Hong Kong

Michael Neugebauer Publishing Ltd.,
Unit 28, 5/F, Metro Centre, Phase 2,
No.21 Lam Hing Street, Kowloon Bay, Kowloon, Hong Kong.
Phone: +852 2807 1711, e-mail: info@minedition.com
This book was printed in May 2017 at L.Rex Ltd
3/F, Blue Box Factory Building, 25 Hing Wo Street,
Tin Wan, Aberdeen, Hong Kong, China
Typesetting in NuevaMM
Color separations by Pixelstorm, Vienna.
Library of Congress Cataloging-in-Publication Data
available upon request.

ISBN 978-988-8341-21-4
10 9 8 7 6 5 4 3 2 1
First impression

For more information please visit our website: www.minedition.com

KNISTER

Sweet Dreams, Bruno

with pictures by Eve Tharlet
translated by Kathryn Bishop

minedition

Bruno, the little marmot, was playing with his friends in the meadow. But Bruno was tired and a little grumpy. He knew it was time for his long winter sleep.

"I don't want to sleep!" said Bruno.
"Then why don't you spend the winter with me," said his friend the goat. "I spend the whole winter climbing up and down the mountains and jumping over rocks."

"It's slippery on those snowy rocks," said Bruno. "I'm afraid that's not for me."

"You could spend the winter with me,"
said the jackdaw, fluttering up to her cozy
nest high above.

"It's much too high for me," said Bruno. "Getting up and
down would be a problem. How would I manage?"

The little mouse said, "Spend the winter with me in the farmhouse! I'm good at sneaking food, I could teach you."

"But there are cats in the farmhouse. And..."
said Bruno meekly, "I'm afraid of their claws."

"Well, then you must spend the winter with me,"
said the hare. "It's such fun to romp through the snow
in winter fur!"

Bruno shivered at the thought.
"I don't grow a warm winter coat like you. I would freeze."

"Come fly with us! We spend the winter in Africa. It's warm there," said the swallow.

Bruno just shook his head. "But I can't fly," he said.

Bruno sighed and yawned.
"I guess everyone spends winter in their own way. For a marmot hibernation is the best."

"Sweet dreams, Bruno!"
Bruno said goodbye to his friends and playmates, crawled through his tunnel and nestled in his cozy den to sleep.

"We're so different, but we're real friends," he mumbled and fell straight to sleep.

His sleep was full of dreams, and he did such exciting things. Anything is possible in dreams.

Bruno jumped with the goat over the rocks,
from one mountain to the next.
Hooray!

How lovely to dream of floating to
the nest of the jackdaw.
Amazing!

Bruno dreamed
he even went
cat hunting with
the mouse!
Woo-hoo!

He also dreamed of slipping and sliding in the fluffy white snow with the hare.
Yippee!

And in his dreams, Bruno flew with the swallows high in the sky.

Wow!

"Bruno! Bruno! Bruno!"
These weren't dream-voices he heard now, they were real! Bruno crawled out of his burrow as fast as he could. Spring's warm sunbeams tickled his nose, and best of all, his friends were there waiting for him. "Hello, sleepyhead," said the hare, "no more lazing about. You slept all winter."

"But I was busy in my dreams," said Bruno as he stretched and yawned. "We did the most incredible things together."

"And now I'm ready!" He was so glad that he had the whole long summer to spend with his friends.